John Vlachos is an art instructor, artist and author and has cultivated his craft to a high art form. His concern for decency, respect and integrity is mirrored in his writing the 'Nero in the Land of Nut' trilogy.

JOHN VLACHOS

NERO
and the
SOCIAL AGREEMENT

AUSTIN MACAULEY PUBLISHERS™
LONDON • CAMBRIDGE • NEW YORK • SHARJAH

Ordering Information

Quantity sales: Special discounts are available on quantity purchases by corporations, associations, and others. For details, contact the publisher at the address below.

Publisher's Cataloging-in-Publication data

Vlachos, John
Nero and the Social Agreement

ISBN 9798891557321 (Paperback)
ISBN 9798891557338 (ePub e-book)

Library of Congress Control Number: 2024910066

www.austinmacauley.com/us

First Published 2024
Austin Macauley Publishers LLC
40 Wall Street, 33rd Floor, Suite 3302
New York, NY 10005
USA

mail-usa@austinmacauley.com
+1 (646) 5125767

I dedicate this book to all the friends who have cheered me when I was down, and to all those who believed in me when I didn't believe in me, and to those who have become beacons of flame and inspiration throughout my life and made of it a good life, a life full of interest and fascination. I owe more than I can possibly give back. This book is my gift to all those noble people called friends.

Chapter One
...And They Came Back

Once upon a curious time, the little boy Nero, who lived in the land of Nut and was from Nutville, had just come back after a long and dangerous journey. He had taken Nora Nunnians with him, who also brought her little dog Noodles in the basket of nuts and knitters. Apparently, they believed they would become nutless if they reached the formidable Nutless Forest, where, it was said, there were no nuts.

This had all been Nero's idea, of course, and what it really meant, nobody ever knew. It was not explained. It was just the way it was always said, and this made it very nysterious. When Nero heard about it, he was immediately nintrigued. The nystery drew him further and further, closer and closer to the formidable Nutless Forest. Why there were no nuts there could've meant that no nut trees grew there, or that ordinary-minded people never lived there.

It certainly couldn't mean you would become nutless if you went there because... what would make you nutless if you were already a nut? The idea of nutlessness could not have ever meant anything to a forest anyway. And simply having the title of the formidable Nutless Forest was not enough to exorcise a living nut into becoming nutless. The argument had no logic in it.

There was nothing nutty or nutless about it. It simply had nothing to do with the idea of being nuts, so how could Nero have ever believed it? Was it because, at that moment, he was nuts after all?

Nero and Nora Nunnians, with Noodles in the basket of nuts and knitters, had become convinced it was worth the effort. They traveled far and wide, meeting various characters all along the way and visiting places they had never been before.

The journey for nutlessness changed them completely when they reached the formidable Nutless Forest.

Just as they were sure they would finally become nutless, to their surprise, they discovered they were never nuts, according to the ancient trees that told them so, and that the whole meaning of their enterprise lay in the journey itself. If that wasn't nuts to begin with!

Isn't it wonderful to discover such things? Isn't it nexquisite to learn so much from a journey? Nero thought so, and so did Nora and Noodles in the basket of nuts and knitters.

It was all so simple to them, and they celebrated with the animals and sang songs of joy all the way back home. When they reached Nutland, they shared the things they had learned from all the different characters they had met and proved to all of Nutville that they were not nuts.

This, of course, set the people of Nutville talking and whispering behind closed doors. There was a storm brewing. Unbeknownst to our friends Nero and Nora with Noodles in the basket of nuts and knitters, they had set off a chain reaction throughout Nutland, and all the people rose up to meet this challenge. How could they claim such a thing, they thought? It was known all round that people in Nutville were nuts.

A notion of impossible things!

That was their hallmark, or so it was said. Now here was a little boy and little girl claiming to take that away from them; claiming they had discovered they were never nuts to begin with.

Hodgepodge! It was naughty and natty of them, full of a ninny of silly things. It was equivalent to an ailing squirrel's stomach—unheard of! It was notful and natful and didn't make sense to anyone's noggin. The whole notion was daft and quite avant-garde. Nothing could be less nelectable, or netrievable. It was all such a ridiculous notion of impossible things.

It rivaled stupidity and nipidity, napidity and nanipidy, and caused total mayhem. It was an unacceptable babble of words and an atrocious way to think.

The very thinking of it was thoughtless, if thinking was in the mix, and no miniscule thought had been put into it. It obviously had not been thought out, or at least not enough to make it a thought at all, and any thinking that went on was completely thoughtless. It was very disturbing to suddenly be called nutless. It grated against the status quo.

It challenged the Social Agreement! This was a very nerious issue and it issued forth with all the aplomb of an idiot. What would happen to their neputation? Tourists came from all over the world to see how nuts they were, how nutty they acted, and how royally ludicrous they could behave. The people in Nutville were positively proud of their inherent pedigree in foolishness and fun.

It was about fun, after all, wasn't it? Now you had someone coming along to take it all away. There were different levels of nipidity, and it took great ingenuity to reach napidity.

All the Nutvillers cried out!

The whole notion of one's noggin making it all the way up to nanipidy was almost unheard of and considered quite an accomplishment.

They enjoyed all the applause and notoriety for this and lauded it over their neighbors. They raised their noses high and paraded themselves as ridiculously as they could. It inspired them to be as wacky as one could get, as pointlessly absurd and infinitesimally mad to the point of idiocy and other related insecurities.

The nutty people of Nutville had raised the bar and transformed craziness into an art form. This was no small achievement, and they were not about to have it all torn down by these two upstarts.

There was no end to how far they would go, even to court if they had to. There had to be a law that made it illegal to have your pedigree challenged. Nonetheless, it was not nutsense to them, even though the whole thing was nutsense.

Nutsensical or not, it was nanootless to say the least.

No one could convince them they were nutless because they had been born in Nutville. Imagine that. That qualified their nindentials. That made them nuts. They considered themselves a special species of people. To the people of Nutland, the name of their town said it all. One wonders what would've happened if the name was ever changed, for instance, to Nutlessville? Would they immediately consider themselves nutless? Was it all in the name? Was it in one's title that determined what and who you were? Was that what it was all about? Was the status quo so important that it became irreverent to change it? Now, that was a lot to think about and certainly too many questions. Even poor Noodles, in the basket of nuts and knitters, acquiesced under the effort to understand it.

"I don't understand what all the fuss is about," said Nero to Nora, who was holding Noodles in the basket of nuts and knitters. "What's the matter with everybody?" Nora just looked at him, nerturbed, and so did Noodles in the basket of nuts and knitters. She too thought everyone would celebrate the idea of being nutless, since being nuts was so embarrassing. "After all we've been through to prove we are not nuts and never have been, they don't want to face it," said Nora. "The trees told us so, didn't they, Nero? Didn't they say we were never nuts to begin with and how foolish it was to think so? Didn't they send us on our way happy?" Nora looked at Nero for nonfidence, the nonfidence that they were right and that the whole town had gone bonkers with this idea of being nuts with pedigree.

She thought "pedigree" referred to dogs like Noodles in the basket of nuts and knitters, not people. Noodles thought "pedigree" referred personally to him too. Were they going to take that away from him? It was all getting quite nanfusing indeed.

It was as natty and naughty as it could get. It was diabolically nipid and ninsternian and downright natful to be of any help to anyone. No one and nothing could nipper or noppy it back together. The whole thing was naniperous and absolutely noxious to the ethers in one's body and mind. One nained and noined to try to figure it out. Nora was nanspersed with worry and Nero felt nundriad. It all came down to a head one day when the townspeople came knocking on Nero's door.

He and Nora were giving Noodles a bath when they heard a great commotion outside and the door being banged on.

Noodles barked in panic, and he scampered to find his basket of nuts and knitters. "None to worry," said Nero to Nora as he marched with ninsternian confidence. "You are being noxious and nascent nincompoops, all of you," exclaimed Nero upon opening the door. "You are acting like naniput ninnys and nambuctious clowns. You should be ashamed of yourselves. Instead of being liberated from the insipid stigma of being considered nuts and ridiculed by the world, you wallow in your own ignorant numbness and silly williness, and double billiness. But I will not be nained and noined into believing it, nor will I be it… whatever it is." That was an important question. What was it?

How many things were they talking about, or were they talking about one thing only? Were they talking about anything at all? Anything in particular? It was hard to say after so much nanolyzing.

After nipiting and napiting, and nanferous ninnying, after nanosizing and noodling, noverteen and nagging nanpooing, it was all becoming quite clear.

To Nero, it was cut and dry. No one in Nutville was nuts just because their town was titled that way. The townspeople tried to understand his logic because they lost track of what they were talking about anyway. Did their town once grow nut trees but no longer did? Was that where the name came from? Did that mean they were not nuts after all? How would that affect the tourist industry? The whole thing was sounding nuttier by the hour.

Their shouts dwindled down to murmurs and whispers of claims and disclaimers and something about pedigree no one understood… and whose idea was that anyway?

Then there was the nanosizing noodling and the idea of everyone possibly not being nuts, but what did that mean? …and they would ask Nora, but Nora always turned to Nero who seemed to have the final word, unless you count Noodles whimpering in the basket of nuts and knitters, still wet from his interrupted bath.

It went on this way in Nutville until things settled down. Slowly the Nutvillers began to get used to the idea that they were not nuts after all. Nero was successful in convincing them because they had it from the horse's mouth, as they say. The great ancient trees had said so, and if they said it… well, it had to be so on account of their great wisdom and humble demeanor. On account of their title and station in the scheme of things, and because the Social Agreement had it written down on stone, as they say. Although Nero was hard-pressed to find any stone in the vicinity.

Having come from a horse's mouth as they say!

In this way, many things were said and assumed and believed in… since it had come from a horse's mouth… on account of the status quo, and the fingers pointing to whom and what situation of great and small complexity. On account of who was who, and what was what. On account of indiscretions and misdemeanors, and all sorts of things taken for granted that before were not accepted, but now were, and on account of all these changes and having come from a horse's mouth… it was suddenly possible for them to believe they were not nuts. All this on account, and all from a horse's mouth. "It sure took a lot to convince them, didn't it?" inquired Nora to Nero one day as they sat outside on the porch. Noodles was chasing a squirrel. Nero agreed as he counted in his head all the accounts mentioned in the above. He could not understand why it had become so complicated. It seemed the Nutvillers loved to get complicated and confused. They enjoyed the idea of accounts written down in stone, even if no stone was ever found, and what was what and what not in the scheme of things. Yet, Nero could not get something out of his mind, and Nora couldn't get it out of her mind either. Noodles couldn't even consider it, as he nuggled back into his basket of nuts and knitters.

Something was amiss. Nero and Nora looked at each other. To them both, it all sounded a bit nutty and brought back memories of how things used to be. Had anything changed at all? Had noting down the particulars brought a better situation to the situation? The notes had been noted, the nains and noins had been counted, and all the ninternal nanfusions were brought to bear, balancing an imbalance in the scheme of things. But why did it still resemble silliness in all its glory, and why had nuttiness reached a new level of imbecility?

Licorice houses

Something had to be done. Nero thought and thought as the sun set slowly across the sky. The shadows of the trees and houses got longer and longer until they resembled stretched licorice.

Nora tried to look like she was thinking, but in fact, she didn't know what she was supposed to be thinking about. Whatever it was she couldn't get out of her mind before had completely escaped her mind now. Noodles, on the other hand… well. It completely fell on Nero's shoulders to come up with a plan that would make things right… whatever that meant. He just wasn't convinced that Nutvillers were not nuts. They seemed to be acting nuttier and nuttier when trying to act nutless.

Was being nutless an act? Were they really nuts after all, but acting nutless? Did they even know what was happening? He had to do something to rectify, salvage, rescue, and reclaim. He had to regain, recuperate, and convalesce, and improve this dire situation. He had to call out the alarm and send out a blast exclaiming the news. He had to trumpet forth whatever it was. He had to announce, he had to declare, he had to bellow out and make known the argument. He had to take matters into his own hands without spilling anything. He had to go around the village and ask people about this. He just had to. And, of course, he didn't know why.

It was always that way. Not knowing exactly what you have to do and what not to do. And what about how things tended to get mixed up, and people stepping on other people's feet as they say, and how easy it was to insult others, without even trying to, but just doing it anyway and not knowing why they react the way they do and… oh darn!

Sending out a blast!

Nero felt he was never going to get it right, and this mission of his was feeling harder than the long, dangerous journey to the formidable Nutless Forest had been.

Finding anything out wasn't easy. He had learned his lesson the first time around, and now it would be a second time trying. Nero had learned that things were far more complicated and serious, and extremely deep, and enormously wide, and immeasurably tall, and grossly unsure, and habitually doubtful, and horrendously shy, and embarrassing willy-nilly feelings of silliness. These were all very disturbing things he did not need at the moment, and he cast his glance around to see if there was a waste bin he could throw them in. But there wasn't.

Because there wasn't a waste bin, he would have to contend with all of these insecurities, but how easy it would have been if there had been a waste bin to throw them in. How different things would feel. He would not have to face up to the immeasurably tall or the enormously wide things. He would not have to deal with the complicated and the serious, or put up with the grossly unsure, habitually doubtful, or horrendously shy. He knew he could then easily deal with the embarrassing willy-nilly, and he would not in the end feel silly. But there was no garbage bin around. He would have to contend to all of them as he made his way through Nutville.

Another cup of tea as they say!

His mission would be to convince people once and for all that they were never born nuts or are considered nuts, because their village is called Nutville, and make it stick. He had to see them acting normal, like the rest of the world and not be nuts. Of course, acting normal was another cup of tea, as they say, although it really had nothing to do with tea. It was just a figure of speech, as they say, although where the figure comes in Nero never understood.

Being normal opened up another can of worms, as they say, although Nero never understood what role worms played in a can. The more he thought about it, the more confused he became, until it was almost impossible to think at all. Nora suggested he take a break from thinking. "Take a break from thinking about what is or is not normal, Nero," said Nora. Nero thought about taking a break from thinking, but he felt he first had to solve the problem of what was normal. He had to do this if he was going to go out into Nutville and make his rounds.

He had to know what normal was before he could argue the point, didn't he? He had to know what was considered nuts and what wasn't. He had to know what role worms played in a can and how normal was another cup of tea, as they say, even though it had nothing to do with tea proper. He had to familiarize himself with a figure of speech and how a figure can be of any effect in a speech… whatever that was. Even something coming from a horse's mouth seemed complicated. He had to do all this before he could take a break from thinking.

He turned and told this to Nora. Nora thought about it too, but her thoughts were limited to guessing Nero's thoughts. Noodles' thoughts were even fewer than Nora's. It was all so geometrical.

It was so geometrical

These are figures of speech, as they say!

Chapter Two
Making the Rounds

At this point, let us pause, as Nero did, to think about what it was that had to be understood before he had to contend with what things came out of horse's mouths, and cups of tea that didn't mean tea at all, and figures of speech that didn't seem to figure out anything in particular. Nero struggled to understand unclear and misunderstood things. He had to comprehend the grossly unsure and habitually doubtful. He had to confront the immeasurably tall and horrendously shy of situations, which slid into embarrassing willy-nilly feelings of silly actuations.

Of course, all this would not be a problem had he had a waste bin to throw them in. But there was no waste bin around, and he had to tend to these problems when he made his rounds to confront the Nutvillers and press them to the test. After all, his long, dangerous journey to the formidable Nutless Forest must not have happened in vain. He had brought home the bacon, as they say, although again, Nero was hard-pressed to see any connection bacon had to the situation. All he knew was that he had brought them a new wisdom which liberated them from their former selves. As far as these sayings were concerned, he had had enough of them. Now Nutvillers could stand immeasurably tall and feel enormously wide in their pride.

They did not have to be grossly unsure or habitually doubtful anymore. They could feel as interesting and complex individuals with extremely deep and serious thoughts. That is the way he would put it! Now he knew how all these things connected and would become new standards of behavior.

They would no longer be a show for the rest of the world to mock. Nutvillers would have their own destiny and forge a new way of being, that had nothing to do with being nuts. The day would come when being nuts was a thing of the past, and no one would remember how to be nuts anymore. Perhaps he could suggest they change the name of Nutville to Smart Ville. They would certainly be looked up to then.

Now Nero was ready, and he went to Nora and asked her if she would join him on his mission to make the rounds. Nora jumped at the chance to do anything with Nero, because Nero had never been nuts to begin with, and this helped her become nutless too, and it helped Noodles in the basket of nuts and knitters become nutless as well. It was all working out fine, and she felt they would succeed in convincing everyone they were nutless and had never been nuts at all. Needless to say, they had no idea how difficult it was going to be.

Skipping through the poppy field and the raven!

They picked a fine sunny day with a balmy breeze blowing from the north, cool and refreshing and just perfect for what they had to do. Off they went with their basket of nuts and knitters full of delicious nelectables ready for a picnic. Noodles followed close behind. As they picked their way over a field of tall wild grass sprinkled with poppies, Nora got drowsy and suggested to Nero they take a break. "After all," she said, "we are not in a rush, are we? It's not like we are going on a long, dangerous journey anymore." And she was right.

As they sat down amongst the poppies, chewing on some nelectables, a big black raven came fluttering down quite near them. He cooed and cawed at them very loudly.

Nero and Nora thought he was being quite rude, and they tried to shoo him away, but he wouldn't budge. Noodles thought he was being very rude too and barked to get him to go, but the raven wouldn't budge. "Caw! Caw!" he cried in earnest. "You people always do that, always! You are always shooshing me away, as if I am bad company, when I can assure you I am an aristocrat." The raven ruffled its black shiny feathers, preening and prawning its whole body, so its feathers could settle into a flawless form, with a wonderful sheen that shown in the sun, with a certain luster and immaculate nankeen perfection. It certainly did look to have a somewhat raised pedigree, and possibly had been born into a noble family of some merit, but all this was unfamiliar to Nero and Nora and Noodles in the basket of nuts and knitters.

The non-such raven!

A ball of non-suches, indeed!

"An aristocrat?" cried Nero in full doubt about that fact. "How can a common raven be of aristocratic stock, I ask you? You've got some gall rudely disturbing our afternoon repose in this beautiful field of poppies." "Caw! Caw!" exclaimed the raven with more determination than before. "You see this beak? You see how it curves downward ever so slightly toward the tip? That, my boy, has taken millions of years to evolve just so… and the length, notice the elegance of its length as it forms a perfect stylish cone of distilled beauty. Very vogue and very in. That took another million or so years to form. I am a work of art, sir. What are you?"

Nero couldn't believe he was having a conversation with a raven that believed it was of aristocratic stock with pedigree to boot. What could he do with someone like that? How do you deal with a bloated ego? While Nero was busy thinking this out, the raven came closer and closer to the basket of nuts and knitters.

To anyone even remotely aware, the real motive of the raven became clear. All this posturing was a smoke screen to keep Nero and Nora busy, till the raven could lunge for the basket of nuts and knitters and gobble up the nelectables.

But for one moment, the raven forgot to calculate where Noodles was. Noodles was in the basket, ready and waiting to pounce on the raven if the raven tried for the basket. Noodles was nart. He was narter than anyone had bartered for, and this was nelicious of him. Yeh for Noodles!

Let's all root for Noodles! Root for Noodles yeh! I can just imagine it now, imagining Noodles with his tongue sticking out with glee and furiously wagging his little tail in the basket of nuts and knitters, as he hears us rooting for him.

Oh yes and by the way, he does hear us. He knows we're reading the story. Noodles can hear us laughing hysterically because he knows how funny this all reads out. He is happy to be a part of all this happiness and joy. He told me so. He also told me that he thought people the silliest nuttiest creatures of all. Noodles is one of the loved characters and the story wouldn't be the same without him.

Now Nero was beside himself with the raven, although he could never see his double. He suddenly realized what the raven was up to and rose to his feet. The raven was immediately alerted to the fact that his trick had been found out. How absolutely nunnerving and immediately nompelling for a call to arms! What inner panic and detestable feelings of fear and flight and saving one's life; at having been discovered as a dastardly nusillanimous fiend. 'Oh, dear!' thought the raven as he took flight.

"I barely scratched the surface of my pristine deportment. I hardly got the chance to reveal my inner and outer perfection, my disclosed secrets, and my nysteries of life in the altruistic chambers of my heart. They will never know what jewel entered their space, a rare commodity like me they will never experience again. They will never know the plush covering of the indigo thoughts I entertain in my spare time. Oh well, they are the losers. Nusillanimity my foot!" And he flew away never looking back.

"Who did he think he was?" cried Nero to Nora and Noodles in the basket of nuts and knitters.

"How could he think he had perfect deportment?

How dare he believe he had any secrets of importance to divulge, or nysteries, or altruistic allusions of the heart? What heart? Ha, if all commodities came as cheap as him. If all indigo thoughts and emerald ideas could be whipped up in spare times."

Nero was beside himself, although he could never see his double standing there. Nevertheless, he had become livid. Nora had become livid too, even though she never understood what pristine deportment meant, or imagined a cheap commodity. It would help if she knew what a commodity was. She couldn't quite comprehend what indigo thoughts might look like, or emerald ideas really were either. Noodles had a hard time of it too but, pristine deportment and cheap commodities were beyond his grasp.

Nero was a bit nerturbed at how their first outing on their mission had started so negatively. It did not portend a successful mission. Nora tried to understand what nerturbed felt like, and Noodles in the basket of nuts and knitters simply gave up. There was no wrangling it. It was a knotted ball of non-suches. To Nora, the raven was simply a non-such, and she suggested to Nero to see it like that, so they could go on with their mission. Nero thought about it and agreed, so they gathered their things and off they went to meet the citizens of Nutville.

Crossing over Neehi River on Nonsense Bridge!

Noodles didn't understand what they had agreed on, the poor thing, but he acted like he did, so they wouldn't tarry any longer. They crossed the field of poppies, till they reached Ninny Park, and crossed that, till they got to Neehi River where they scampered across Nonsense Bridge. Of course, there was nothing nutsensical about Nonsense Bridge, so it confused them why it had been named that way.

It was common sense to have named the river Neehi because it was deep up to the knees, but there was nothing nutsensical about the bridge. "It just goes to show you how difficult our mission will be Nora," said Nero looking a little glum. "The Nutvillers have given everything in our town nutty names because they believe their nuttiness is genuine. Isn't that the nuttiest thing of all?" Nora couldn't say because the idea of questioning the issue seemed even nuttier and completely scattered her mind.

Noodles, in the basket of nuts and knitters, on the other hand, couldn't get the question, the issue, or the nuttiness. He simply couldn't get anything right, especially on the other hand. As far as a scattered mind was concerned, that was normal for him. Then Nora suggested all these funny names might have to do with the tourist industry. But that went over Nero's head completely.

Upon crossing the bridge, the first persons they met were Mr. and Mrs. Nample. They seemed to be walking towards No Way Crescent where Nappy Nippers Variety store was. Nappy Nippers had been there for ages and was a well-known traditional establishment. Everyone shopped for something or other everyday there, so it was no surprise to see two citizens going to shop there. They saw Nero and Nora carrying Noodles in a basket of nuts and knitters, and slightly bowed their heads in respect. Just as they were going to pass them Nero stepped in front of them to say something.

Mr. and Mrs. Nample

Mr. Nample said, "Good morning to you young ones," as he took his tall hat off. Mrs. Nample smiled. They were exceedingly cheery and extremely agreeable people. Their whole deportment was one of complete positiveness and an exceptionally, remarkably, surprisingly delicate constitution. "Good morning to you too," said Nero with as much aplomb as he could muster. Nora tried with all her might to show as much of a delicate constitution as she could too, and Noodles almost came out of his skin trying to accomplish it.

"We would like to ask you a few questions if you don't mind, Mr. and Mrs. Nample. There's so much to be said about the nuttiness issue and…" Mr. and Mrs. Nample looked at each other. Mr. Nample interrupted, "Nuttiness issue? What nuttiness issue, my boy? I thought we had squared the T's and dotted the I's on this one. Surely Nutvillers are as free from nuttiness as one could be. After all the concept is all in the mind, isn't it? It is a concept, isn't it? And it is all in the mind, yes? That's what you said, didn't you?"

Nero looked at Nora in surprise. Nora was struggling with the nuttiness issue and having an extraordinarily difficult time with squaring T's and dotting I's. She couldn't see T's or I's anywhere. The fact there was a strange concept in the mind, floating somewhere in there, and that they should all be paying attention to it totally dissembled her. She couldn't comprehend all this symbolism, but she did remember they had set out for something. But with all this stuff suddenly floating around in her mind, she had forgotten. Noodles, on the other hand, was chewing his bone blissfully in the basket of nuts and knitters. To Nero, it looked like their mission had already succeeded. Until Mrs. Nample opened her mouth.

"Dear, oh dear, what do we have here?" said Mrs. Nample. "Must we always be talking about this silly thing? How silly does it have to get before we are through with it? Maybe it has to get through with us. I have lived in Nutville all my life, young man, and I swear, it's getting sillier and sillier, nuttier and nuttier ever since this concept of nuttiness became an issue. Before we were simply nuts for the tourist industry, now we have to disprove it. To have to disprove you are nuts is the nuttiest of nutty things."

She turned to Mr. Nample, all flushed and disturbed in her comfort zone.

Nero knew immediately that nuttiness reigned supreme in Nutville. They had their work cut out for them. It wasn't as cut and dry as Mr. Nample had made it seem. It wasn't as easy as one two three. The T's may have been crossed and the I's dotted, but by Jove, nothing had really changed in Nutville. He nudged Nora so she could see it too, but Nora was profoundly nanfused indeed, and Noodles in the basket of nuts and knitters was sent flying through the universe with his nanfusion.

Looking at Mrs. Nample, Nero said, "Yes, Mrs. Nample, I understand how you might see it like that, but no one ever asked you to disprove you are nuts. The idea is to be nutless. I am here to prove to you that all of you are not nuts. No matter how nutty it all sounds, not nuts is better than nuts." Mrs. Nample replied, "Young man, can't you put this aside for once and just live here in peace and quiet? Being nuts or not being nuts… is that the question? What have we come to? What does it matter who is what and for what reason? If Nutvillers want to be nuts then let them. Why should you have to prove anything else?"

And she turned to Mr. Nample and said, "Come along, Harry, we've got shopping to do!" And off they went as fast as they could under the circumstances. Nero kept being beside himself. Again, and again no matter how many times he looked; he could not find a second Nero standing beside him. Then why did the expression exist? He wondered.

He would have to deal with that some other time. He just got angrier and angrier and more and more frustrated. He would not be nained or noined. He had to be persistent in his endeavor to prove the nutlessness of these nutty people. But the Social Agreement would not let him. Nero had to tackle this before he could prove his point. He realized it was what had been agreed upon that won the day. So how could he change the agreement? How had it been made in the first place? He would find this Mr. Agreement. Nero had to take a few steps back before he could go forward.

He turned to Nora and said, "Nora, this isn't getting us anywhere. We have to go back a few steps before we can go forward." Nora inquired, "What? What is this now, Nero? Haven't we got enough to deal with? Now you want to add to our problems. Don't forget, there is the problem of crossing the T's and dotting the I's. There are one, two, three numbers which I'll never understand. There is the strange concept called 'the issue' floating in our heads seemingly lost, even to itself, and what about all the symbolism swimming around and tampering with everything? Proving and disproving nuttiness isn't helping matters and turning it into a question makes it worse. Now you want to tackle someone called Mr. Social Agreement that has to be found, by taking so many steps back, in order to proceed forward. Do we even know what he looks like?

I'm not at all certain you are taking the right course, and if you are, it seems too much for little you to handle. Taking it all in one fell swoop, I would say we are behaving nuttier than any Nutviller ever has." Nora was out of breath. To Nero, it was more obvious. He had to find Mr. Social Agreement and wrestle him to the ground. If only he knew where to look. You see, he was invisible to the naked eye. What a nilemma he was in. 'Gracious to Betsy,' as they say, although Nero had never met Betsy.

Nero and Nora continued on their way through Nutville meeting various people. Nero was adamant about all this searching for Mr. Social Agreement. He actually became obsessed, and he was determined to give him a piece of his mind when he found him. Who did he think he was, this Social Agreement? With what official potting and patting did he make decisions, and how could he dictate this or that, swing things around in nutsensical tirades, and forge new alliances to get his way? Nero had to meet this Social Agreement and put him in his place. He had governed Nutville for too long, and it was high time things changed around here.

Mr. Nymes

It wasn't long before they met Mr. Nymes walking down Nolpole Street. Nero bowed slightly and began a conversation with him. Mr. Nymes seemed quite jolly to oblige him. "Mr. Nymes, how do you do, sir?" said Nero hesitatingly, considering how it had played out with Mr. and Mrs. Nample. "I just want to ask you a question. Do you know where I can find Mr. Social Agreement?" Mr. Nymes just stared at him in disbelief. "You see, I have to find him because it's very important. He's sabotaging all my efforts to prove to all of Nutvillers that they're not nuts." Mr. Nymes still kept staring at Nero in an extraordinary way.

"Son," said Mr. Nymes finally, "are you sure you have your facts straight?" Nero just stared at Mr. Nymes in disbelief. Then he said, "Why, I am sure I don't know what you mean." Mr. Nymes stared at him again. "You are not sure what I mean? Don't you mean it's the other way around?" "Well now look here, Mr. Nymes, if we keep this up I'll positively get dizzy," exclaimed poor Nero, desperate to comprehend. He glanced at Nora for some assistance, but she was in some type of trance from all the rollie-pollie conversation ollie. Noodles, in the basket of nuts and knitters, was already simply rolling around unabashedly, having given up long ago and just coming along for the ride.

Nero was beside himself once again, but this time he didn't even bother to try and find his other self. Why was Mr. Nymes so difficult? He thought. "Mr. Nymes, I take it you don't know where Mr. Social Agreement is? I'm having a terrible time trying to find him and no one seems to know of his whereabouts." "Nero, my boy," said Mr. Nymes, "I don't know what you mean. Dear boy, look at me. Have you gone bonkers? It's a rule of thumb, as they say, my boy, there is no Mr. Social Agreement."

There is no Mr. Social Agreement!

It's a rule of thumbs!

That knocked Nero into another universe.

Nero suddenly stood to attention. What rule of thumb? He thought. For one instant, he heard the little man inside his head warning of subterfuge. If there was no Mr. Social Agreement, then where did the agreement among the Nutvillers come from? He thought. He stared at Mr. Nymes rather suspiciously. "You wouldn't be pulling my leg now, would you, Mr. Nymes? If there isn't anyone called Mr. Social, what's the agreement all about?" Mr. Nymes could only look at Nero with worry.

What trouble had he gotten himself into? He thought. What do you answer a delusional boy who thinks an agreement is a person? And where did he get that idea? He thought.

"My boy, I think I know what your problem is. Little Nero, you are simply confused and need to get your facts cross-referenced. You will never find the Social Agreement in the way you're looking for it. It's an unspoken rule among all the citizens of Nutville; a silent agreement defining the status quo, the standard by which we all behave, so as not to step on people's feet; so as not to insult, on account of respect and civility, on account of understanding and good manners and listening to the little man inside your head, on account of paying attention to what is being said, as a rule of thumb, as they say, although no thumbs are used to make rules."

It was at this point Nero glanced at Nora. She seemed to have gone into mental shock. The cross-referenced facts didn't help. The continuous bombardment of nintercious ninformation totally dissembled her.

She was in no position to be of any help. Noodles in the basket of nuts and knitters was also disassembled. What made poor Nora go into shock was the realization of how far they had slid into nuttiness.

It was almost embarrassing to watch her dear Nero make blunder after blunder in this affair with Mr. Social Agreement, who wasn't a person at all, but a thing on account of the status quo, on account of respect and civility and good manners, on account of the little man in our heads and that thumbs were not used to make rules.

To Nora, the most nerplexing part of all this was the little man in our heads. She was not aware of such a creature. And if we were to listen to what he had to say, who did he listen to? Another little man in his head? And did it continue this way infinitum? What was going on?

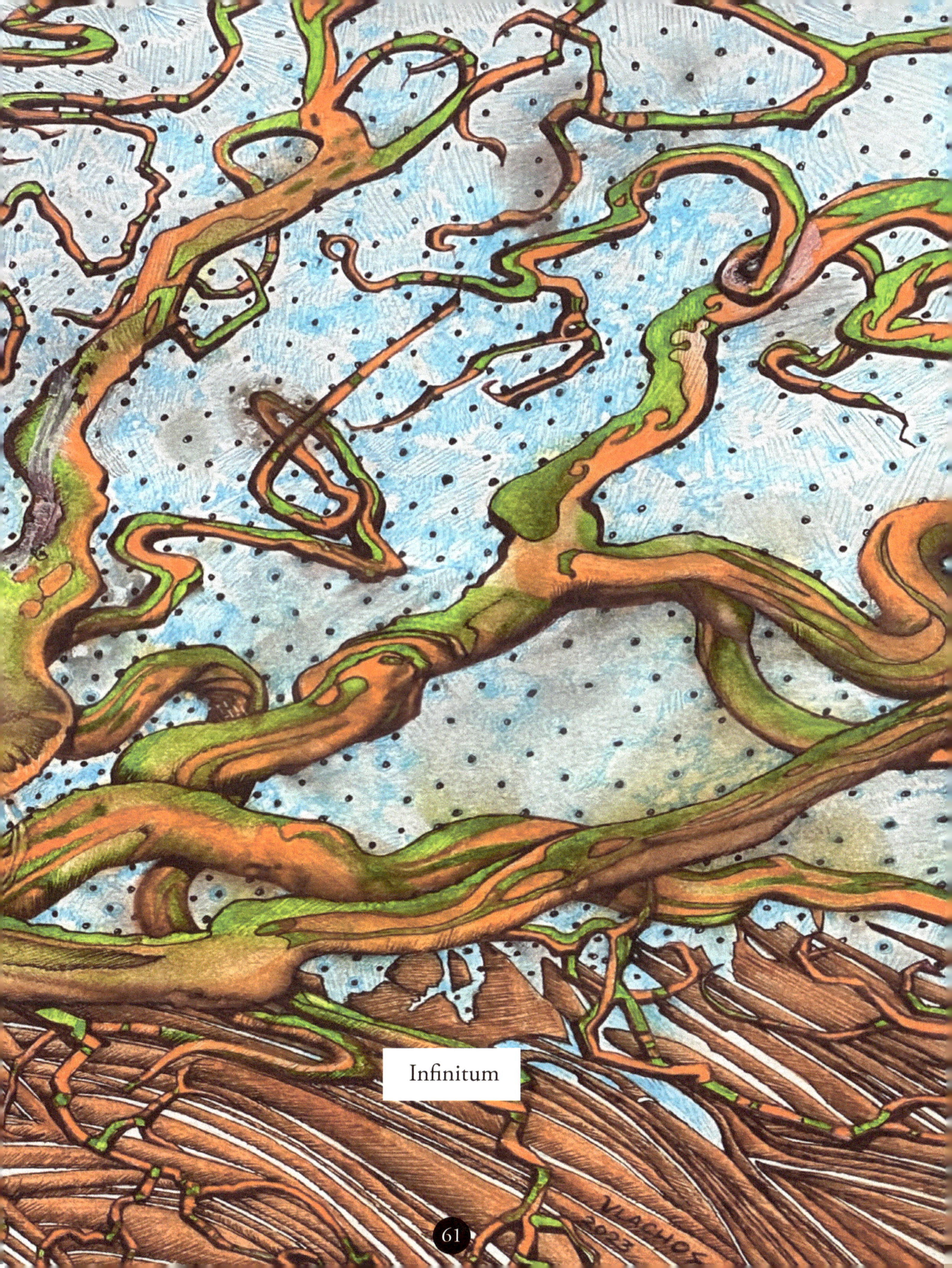
Infinitum

This totally noggled her mind as she tried to escape into the basket of nuts and knitters with Noodles, who was also nonboozeled. "Nothing, nothing, nothing at all!" cried Nora in her nelirium. "It's always about nothing in the end, Nero, and I wonder if it's all worth it." Poor girl doesn't know what she is saying, thought Nero. He looked again at Mr. Nymes and thanked him for his enlightening information. Then, they set off once again to meet other people in Nutville.

So far, it was turning out to be very interesting, thought Nero. At least he was getting to the bottom of the Social Agreement issue. No wonder he couldn't find it; it was invisible. It wasn't a person; it was a status quo. He felt a little silly just thinking about it. "And to think I thought it was a person, ha!" laughed Nero in his nisbelief. For the first time in a long time, Nero saw that being nutty could actually be fun. Was that why there was an agreement between the townspeople of Nutville? He thought. Was there something he was missing? Could Nora, even in her nelirium, possibly be right when she suggested it wasn't worth it?

Slowly but surely, Nero began going through a transformation. It was a nonvelation. Nonetheless, he still had to sift through other discrepancies that confused him. There was what came out of a horse's mouth, which everyone accepted as fact. He personally had never heard a horse say anything, but he wouldn't put it past it if it did. It couldn't be stranger than thumbs being used to make rules or the little man in our heads. Cross-referenced facts were another gross miscalculation on his part. Nero never calculated cross-referenced facts to play a role in the issue of any agreement at all. Why Mr. Nymes would bring it up he would never understand. Why would you need to cross-reference anything? He thought. He had so much to learn.

Mr. Nymes mentioned several accounts being considered. What were they all about? On account of this and on account of that… on account of manners and civility, he had said. On account of not stepping on people's feet, he had said. It was a silent agreement to monitor human behavior. Really? Thought Nero.

By now he had reached the point where he had to ask some very important questions. As they had already tipped their hats to Mr. Nymes, it didn't take long before they encountered Mrs. Nether, who ran a nursery on Nanny Drive, of course. Now Mrs. Nether was just popping over to Nelly Nancy's Nippy knits store to buy some knitting needles because hers had snapped in two. Meanwhile, she had left Nola Nines and Nishi Niv in charge of the nursery in her absence. There were some other girls there as well, but they don't all have to be mentioned.

Nero started walking beside Mrs. Nether. He had to walk rather briskly to keep up because Mrs. Nether was in a hurry, apparently to get back to her nursery. "Greetings Mrs. Nether, how do you do?" asked Nero very cordially. Mrs. Nether was a little startled at how quickly Nero suddenly appeared. She hadn't noticed him in the vicinity. "Well, what are you up to, young man? Have you recovered from your long dangerous journey yet? We are all so pleased for your safe return and all the wonderful, good news you brought with you, although all of us were a bit skeptical at first." Mrs. Nether liked to talk and seemed to have the gift of the gab, as they say. Of course, Nero could never understand what that meant either. He could never put two and two together to see how they were related. Besides. what kind of gift would gabbing make?

Mrs. Nether's splendid aplomb

Mrs. Nether continued, "Many of the townspeople still can't understand what all the fuss was about. All this talk of nuts and nuttier as opposed to not nuts and nutless. It's all too confusing for me, and I never thought about it at all before. No one in Nutville thinks about it either."

She paused to take a breath, "We are the town of Nutvillers, and that's as simple as it gets." Nero smiled, almost delighted at her convivial nature and splendid aplomb. Maybe he could ask Mrs. Nether his questions, he thought. "Mrs. Nether, may I ask you some questions that are very important for the research I am doing?" he inquired boldly but politely. Mrs. Nether was all ears, as they say. We won't say anything to Nero about this because it will drive him crazy. Nero saw she was ready to hear him out and he said, "I am using my square noggin to do round things. It's not easy, mind you, but I'm trying to bring all the loose ends together in a neat circle."

Mrs. Nether stared at him somewhat like Mr. Nymes had done, which caught Nero off guard. "Excuse me," asked Mrs. Nether, "you are using your square noggin to circle an argument? Since when have noggins evolved into squares and how do you circle a proposal?" Then she added, "Why don't you just use your round noggin to make all your round research easier? After all, it's in your round head." She looked rather proud of herself as they entered Novel Street on their way to New Street where Nelly Nancy's Nippy Knits store was. Nero had never thought of his thinking as round but square because he was a boy and not a girl. He had been told this by Uncle Ninny, who said men think squarely while women think roundly. It surprised him that Mrs. Nether was not aware of this.

Nora, on the other hand, was listening to what was being discussed, so as not to miss the latest round of idiotic chatter that had been going on ever since they decided to go on this ridiculous trek to nowhere. And nowhere is where it was going, but she was hard-pressed to tell that to Nero.

He was hell-bent on continuing this so-called research mission that had to do with being nuts or nutless because of an invisible Social Agreement, to say the least, on account of human behavior, their civility, and their manners, on account of the status quo mind you, on account of the little man in their heads who may have been listening to a littler man in his head, and because other issues were slowly drifting into the assortment, like thumbs and rules and using the noggin to think in squares and circles, not to mention the dreaded horse's mouth. It was a heady mix making for a very dense atmosphere.

Then Nero put some questions to Mrs. Nether. "At what point had the people of Nutville gotten together to decide on nuttiness as being the norm in Nutville? Why would they agree on such a thing in the first place when they could've agreed to be nutless instead? And why was the Social Agreement invisible?" Poor Mrs. Nether. These were the worst questions she could possibly have been asked, especially in her hurried state. In fact, for anyone in Nutville, they were the worst. Nero seemed to be out of touch with reality. Mrs. Nether stared at him again because it was all she could do to try to show him that something was wrong. However, Nero was blissfully confident doing his research. So much so, he couldn't see the forest from the trees, as they say, but we won't tell him that either.

"Well, young man, how can I put it?" started Mrs. Nether. "First of all, a Social Agreement is an unspoken pact a society makes, and it happens more or less unconsciously. The town never got together for a huge meeting to decide upon it… oh no… it doesn't work that way. It's not quite so cut and dry," said Mrs. Nether in as dignified way as she could. Nero thought about the cut and dry for a while. Nora thought about the unconscious pact, and Noodles in the basket of nuts and knitters didn't think at all.

Mrs. Nether continued, "Now I don't know who ever told you Nutvillers were nuts, but I've never heard of it. We are Nutvillers but it doesn't make us nuts. In fact, it's all for the tourist industry. As for your wondering about the Social Agreement being invisible, it's a pact about the status quo, a mental arrangement not a physical stroll in the park." Mrs. Nether had finally reached Nelly Nancy's Nippy Knits store and excused herself, as she graciously disappeared through the revolving doors in a blaze of glory. "Ta! Ta!" she said, and she was off!

"Well, I'll be darn," exclaimed Nero to Nora as soon as they were alone. "I'll have you know there's more going on here than meets the eye, as they say," and this was something Nero could understand very clearly. "Did you hear that, Nora? What did you make of it?" For the first time in a long time, poor Nora was beside herself too. But she didn't try to find herself because she understood the saying. "Well, let me see," said she to Nero, rather confounded from this new philosophy. "Am I to understand that our trek has no merit? Hmm… I mean the Social Agreement was an unconscious meeting and not a physical stroll through the park. Did you hear that, Nero? How are we going to handle this? There seems to be too much status in the status quo."

Noodles looked at Nero very intently too, as if to say, "You certainly got us in deep water this time, didn't you?"

"Well, Mrs. Nether did mention something about Nutvillers not being nuts," said Nero, "and that's a good sign that our mission has been successful ever since we came back from the formidable Nutless Forest. Perhaps we needn't go on, Nora, as you suggested, since it seems no one believes they are nuts anymore."

To Nora, this whole idea had not felt right from the very start. Now they had discovered an invisible Social Agreement that had never been a person, that had too much status in the status quo, and had been an unconscious act, perhaps by the little man in the square noggin, who listened to another little woman in her round noggin. They had discovered it had all come from a horse's mouth, on account of manners and civility, on account of not stepping on people's feet. There was Nero's supposed nonvelation and on account of cross-referenced facts, thumbs could be used to measure, and other accounts of this and that, which all rounded out to a neat circle.

Nero and Nora felt they had wrapped it up quite nicely, and now clearly understood the said mode. Noodles yelped from happiness at their nonvelation about the said mode, and thought the same thing, although it was to be expected Noodles had not understood anything at all. There was here, here! And there was there, there! And we've done it and now we can go home. It was a gorgeous, porgeous feeling to say the least, and saying less was better than saying more.

Gorgeous porgeous feeling

Nero and Nora started on their way home cheerily enough feeling fairly proud of themselves. Their whole adventure had pressed the issue at hand and revealed there was no danger of Nutvillers becoming nuts ever again.

Of course, when you take into account a cross-referenced fact that Mrs. Nether had suggested, that Nutvillers were never nuts to begin with, and that this was all in Nero's tiny man's noggin who may have been listening to a tinier man in his noggin, it all started to make sense. And what nutsense it made! It was just what the doctor ordered, as they say, although at this point there was no point bringing this to Nero's attention. Nero was not in the right frame of mind, after all that had transpired, to care much about how a doctor fit into the equation with the said mode.

With their trek over, and the research halted about the issue of the Social Agreement, and the status in the status quo, and unconscious meetings in little men's heads who thought squarely about round things, with doctors somehow being involved and how important a horse's mouth could be, on account of this, and on account of that, about cross-referenced facts and the said mode, Nero and Nora called it a day and headed back to their neighborhood near Neehi River where Nonsense Bridge was waiting for them.

It had certainly been an enlightening experience; there was no doubt. It had revealed how ridiculous life could be if you let it. Nero had undoubtedly allowed the element of being nuts to rule the day and had even found fun in it. So, the lesson was, everything was needed for a well-rounded life to be lived.

Nothing should be scoffed at or dismissed before it was tested and cross-referenced. Everything had to be thought out, even if you used a square noggin to bring it all to a neat full circle. Nuttiness was fun and had its place in the world after all, especially in tourism, and all the fuss had been unnecessary. Nora had been right all along, and Nero was going to listen to her more often from now on.

Chapter Three
Off to the Nonastary and Home

Nero and Nora reached Nonsense Bridge, with Nora carrying Noodles in the basket of nuts and knitters. She let Noodles down to play for a while by the banks of the Neehi River. They were all somewhat exhausted from their foray into uncharted territory. It wasn't easy going off on journeys and treks searching for who knows what, and often coming up empty-handed, as they say, although to Nero that would be a disappointment because he always preferred his hands full.

As they paused to recuperate their strength and eat some nuts and knitters, they went down to the bank of the river where Noodles was playing to take a drink from the cold fresh water nushing by. In the distance, Nora could see the Nonastary she went to school when she was even younger than she was now. She remembered she still had friends there. She turned to Nero and suggested they go to the Nonastary since the day was still young just for kicks, as they say.

Nero was not feeling in the kicking mood, except to kick somebody, and said, "Nora, get real. What's at the Nonastary? Who goes to a dumb Nonastary for little spoiled brats that need babysitting?

You wouldn't catch me there in a hundred years!"

Nora was crushed as she took that as a personal affront. It was the first time in their friendship Nero had treated her so carelessly, and thoughtlessly, and dismissively, and flippant, and indifferently, and all the wrong things. She looked at the ground and didn't say anything at all. Her little noggin hurt, and her heart hurt too.

When Nero saw how he had hurt Nora, he was beside himself with pain and regret. Now he knew what it meant to be beside yourself with worry. He looked down at poor Nora sobbing silently and he burst into tears for her. Reaching down to spread his arms around her he cried, "I apologize, my dear Nora, for what I said. I didn't realize there would be consequences. I am such a fool."

Nora immediately recovered. It seems all she needed was to know he hadn't meant it. "You needn't apologize, Nero, 'cause I don't know how to hold an apology. It's invisible, like a Social Agreement. And what are consequences anyway?" Oh, it was so good to have Nora smiling again, thought Nero. So, Nero thought he would play a little trick. "Oh, okay then I take it back," he said. "Take what back?" asked Nora, "does an apology have a shape or does it float in the air like an unconscious agreement?" Nero hadn't thought about an apology in that way before. He was only kidding, of course, but he would have to think about it. Noodles in the basket of nuts and knitters would have to think about it too.

"I don't think an apology is a thing, Nora. It's an intention. An intention is mental and not like a physical walk through the park."

That brought something to mind but he couldn't quite put his finger on it, as they say, although how a finger comes into it he would never know. An apology was a very strange thing, he thought.

And yet, one could offer it and take it back, even though it was invisible and there was nothing to offer or take back. And wasn't that the nuttiest of nutty things? Yes, thought Nero, an apology was the nuttiest Nutland invention he had ever heard of. Then he added as if he just remembered, "As far as consequences are concerned, they are what's left of the actions we take against people."

Nora thought about that. We must be careful then, what we do to people, so we don't hurt them in any way, so there are no consequences, she thought. I must be careful how I treat Nero and Nero has to be careful how he treats me. On account of the consequences, she thought, in her little round mind.

Then Nora looked at Noodles, who was wagging his tail and licking her feet. "I think I must treat animals with as much kindness as I treat people. After all, its common sense, isn't it?" She asked herself, talking to the little girl in her noggin, who probably was talking to her tinier girl in her tiniest noggin. Animals didn't have to think about it. They always treated people nice. Besides, Noodles didn't have a little Noodles thinking for him. So, she had to make sure she never hurt Noodles in any way, and for any reason on account of the consequences. It was fun thinking so many round things, thought Nora.

Then she wondered what it must have felt like to think squarely. On that she could only guess because she was a round little girl and not a square little boy the way boys were.

"Let's go to the Nonastary, Nora, and let's do it right away. You have friends there who will be happy to see you, and you them, and everyone will be overjoyed all around." said Nero eagerly.

Nora looked at Nero in surprise. "But you said you wouldn't be caught there in a hundred years," said Nora, "have they already passed?" Nero chuckled at that. What a clever girl Nora was, he thought. "Come on and stop hesitating. Get up and let's go," he said, gently taking her arm and pulling her up from the river bank, heading for the Nonastary. Off they went to the Nonastary, dancing a jig all the way. Noodles followed close behind, dancing a jig and yelping as well.

Dancing a Jig to the Nonastary

Nora rang a bell that was hanging by a rope just under a canopy of hundreds of hanging roses. At that moment, and at the sound of the bell, countless birds burst in the air like a cloud. It was beautiful here and reminded them of an oasis. Near them, they could hear a gurgling stream nushing by and ninging as it went. "I am happy! I am happy! I am happy!" it kept repeating, over and over again.

Nothing could be cheerier than to hear this little stream ning its nong of joy. It was infectious. It was incorrigible. It was incurable, irresistible, and plainly alluring. It nogged and nigged on its way to the sea and nwisted and nurned with delight. It niggled and naggled, it noogled and noggled and was downright negoggled from its exuberance.

You see, it wasn't enough to be naiged and noiged, nor nattered into a nottered disposition. It couldn't be nottled up or nimited in any way. It wanted to burst its banks from the joy of nushing by in earnest, nilled and nooled so lively, that it nullified any attempts to dull its excitement.

The little stream offered a cool nespite from the heat of the day and there was opulence in its numerosity. There were smiles in every nurgle and winks in every splash. There were twinkling eyes glinting and blinking as drops flew in the breeze. Laughter could be heard with every spray and squirt. Cries of glee were in every misty dewdrop dazzling, sparkling, scintillating, and glistening. Goodness! There were no more adjectives one could use in the English language. The little stream was all of them, and if we wanted to continue to describe it, we would have to change to another language. That won't serve the logistics or cross-referencing of the facts.

The little stream of happiness

The little boys and girls reading this story would no longer understand what they were reading, and we would run into a problem. So, let's just say that the happy little stream was so lovely, it mesmerized Nero and Nora with Noodles in the basket of nuts and knitters, filling their hearts with gladness and delight. There was nothing more for them to do but partake of the good feeling inside.

Let's face it, nothing can surpass partaking of bliss. Absolutely nothing could defeat or cheat, stumble upon, or remonstrate how inclusive the feeling of pure joy can be and becomes utterly undefeatable in the scheme of things. To Nero and Nora with Noodles in the basket of nuts and knitters, nothing could disappoint them. Nothing could naint their wonderful day. They would not get flustered or become nustered, disturbed, or divided, corrupted or undecided, nunstersed or nantided, nothing could spoil the would-be perfect day from becoming decided in the scheme of things. All experiences would flutter like leaves and ninsperse like many seeds into the breeze.

At last, the big, rusted bronze doors creaked open. Someone was opening the door. Someone was watching. Someone was peeking. Someone was trying to think round thoughts with their square noggin. It happened to be a little boy and not a little girl at all. That's why the noggin was producing squareness, according to Nero and his Uncle Ninny. That Uncle Ninny had to be quite a character, thought Nora. He sure spent a lot of time squaring the noggins for boys and rounding the noggins for girls. I wonder what he did in his spare time, thought Nora. Was it one of those things worth finding out, or was it not? She was amused.

Now it was known in all of Nutland that the nuns there had nude fingers. This was a source of contention with the townspeople. They had insisted they wear gloves on account of preferenced noble appearance and a secret political reason. Nora was slightly confused, on account of the fact everyone had nude fingers, but they were not made to wear gloves. Well, the Social Agreement dictated that they were nuns, that's why. The idea was they held a high station, of purpose and poise, of elegance and discretion, disclaiming and obtaining, their rectitude aside, they practiced with integrity, correctness, and well within the status quo. Having studied philosophy and exercising the roundness of their thoughts into ideal circles, there were also other very mysterious reasons nobody understood. But the nuns in the Nonastary were delighted with their gloves.

It was a little boy who opened the door and let them in. He was a very agreeable little boy with agreeability covering him from top to bottom. So cheery was he, that it seemed he had caught the stream's infection. So delightful in every way was he, that smiles formed on all their faces and the clapping of hands could be heard inside. There was music playing too, and a great rounded celebration of sorts was taking place. They could not have come at a better time.

It seemed all the nuns of Nutville had gathered together to partake of their roundness and become circles of nowness, circles of moments, and circles of this and that. It was all about circles of fascination for each other. What a wondrous luxury this was, thought Nora as she mingled in the throng of gaiety and mirth. Who would've ever thought of such a thing? The idea of getting together just to enjoy each other's company had never crossed her mind. 78

She always thought there had to be a reason to get together, like sharing important news, or of an event that was being organized, or some Nutville politician giving a big speech.

Of course, this was very familiar to Noodles in the basket of nuts and knitters because he was always in the state of fascination and never needed reasons of any kind to get together. All the little nuns collected at his feet, smothering him with attention in very round circles. Noodles could feel the round loveliness of their roundness and licked their cheeks with exuberance. Nero, on the other hand, but which hand, had been swept away by the room full of dancing nuns nushing by like the stream outside singing, "We are happy! We are happy! We are happy!

And it seemed they were!

Nora recognized almost all her past friends, but some nuns were newcomers. There was Nally nun and Nola nun, there was Neva, Natty, and Nena nun too. Nancy and Nellie approached Nora and welcomed Nero and Noodles into their circle of friends, as if they had known them all along. It was an exhilarating feeling to be welcomed with open arms, as if everyone had been waiting for their return for years. Nora realized something very important at that moment. Something happened in her heart. Nero realized it too, and Noodles had always known it anyway.

"Nero, I think friends are the most important relations in the world," said Nora unabashedly. "My heart feels like putty, warm and soft and content. It feels it has come home, to a mother, to a father, to an uncle and aunt, to a wrinkled old grandmother who sits by the window waiting for me." Nora plushed. She beamed with a new vitality and knew it was a good idea they visited the Nonastary.

Nero seemed to have rounded off to a perfect circle

"See, Nero, how nice it is here… and you didn't want to come. You assumed before you did your research. You jumped the gun, as they say," said Nora, although there were no guns around.

Nero certainly felt bad about that and regretted it. But the atmosphere was so gay, nothing could touch him now. He was as happy as a lark. He was all wiggly and giggly inside. He could feel a tingling and jingling sensation. He felt a joust and a poust as he joined the gang, dancing a jig and making merry. Nora was too, and so was Noodles in the basket of nuts and knitters, except he wasn't in the basket this time.

Nero did not feel square anymore.

He seemed to have rounded off to a perfect circle. He would forget Uncle Ninny's beliefs about the noggin. Everyone was rounded off to a perfect circle. Everyone was as important as everyone else. Everyone had to take care of everyone. Everyone needed everyone. Everyone was as nutty and not nutty as everyone else, and it had nothing to do with names or titles or Social Agreements. Everything played its part. No one was nuts in Nutville until they were, and until they were not, and it went back and forth like a dance that never stopped.

The day was turning into night and Nero, Nora, and Noodles in the basket of nuts and knitters had to think of going home. Sleep was waiting for them just inside the front door. Their beds were ready to receive them with a sweet embrace and a nuggle and a niggle and a kiss. Tomorrow would see them on a new adventure. And when they woke up, it would be a brand-new day that was singing, "I am happy! I am happy! I am happy!"

And so, it was.

VLACHOS
2022

THE END

Glossary

Nysterious: Mysterious Nintrigued: Intrigued

Nystery: Mystery Nexquisite: Exquisite

Natty: Nasty Ninny: A kid

Notful: unbelieving Natful: Rude

Noggin: Brain Nelectable: Delectable

Netrievable: Irretrievable Nipidity: Stupidity

Napidity: Very stupid Nanipidy: Most stupid

Nerious: Serious Neputation: Reputation

Notoriety: Well-known Nutsensical: Nonsensical

Nindentials: Credentials Nerturbed: Disturbed

Nonfidence: Confidence Nanfusing: Confusing

Nipid: Dumb Nisternian: Foolish

Nipper: Sew Noppy: Glue

Naniperous: Unbelievable Noxious: Feeling sick

Nained: Ignored Noined: Refused

Nanspersed: Frustrated Nundriad: Useless

Nascent Nincompoop: Arrogant Naniput Ninnys: Spoiled kids

Nambuctious: Riotous Numbness: Struck Dumb

Nanolyzing: Analyzing Nipiting Napiting: Searching

Nannosizing Noodling: Scientific Inquiry Nagging Nanpooing: Obstinate

Novertine: Attempting Nuggled: Snuggled

Ninternal: Internal Nanfusions: Details

Nankeen: Absolute Narter: Smarter

Neticious: Delicious Nunerving: Unnerving

Nonpelling: Compelling Nusillanimous: Crafty

Nusillanimity: Conspiring Nerturbed: Disturbed

Nonsuches: Meaningless Nilemma: Dilemma

Nintercious Ninformation: Overkill Nerplexed: Perplexed

Noggled: Baffled Nonboozled: Blown away

Nelirium: Delirium Nisbelief: Disbelief

Nonvelation: Revelation Nushing: Rushing

Nonastary: Monastery Ninging: Ringing

Ning: Ring Nong: Song

Nogged: nodded Nigged: Swayed

Nwisted: Twisted Nurned: Churned

Niggled: Shook Naggled: Bursting

Noogled: Shaking Negoggled: Overjoyed

Naiged: Aware Noiged: Flustered

Nattered: Forced Nottered: Suspicious

Nottled: Bottled up Nimited: Limited

Nilled: Shrilled Nooled: Hummed

Nullified: Cancelled Nespite: Despite

Nurgle: Gurgle Naint: Taint

Nustered: Frazzled Nunstersed: Oblivious

Nantided: Disappointed Ninsperse: Disperse

Plushed: Blushed Nuggle: Snuggle

Niggle: Giggle